¡See You Later, Amigo!
an American border tale

by Peter Laufer
collages by Susan L. Roth

BARRANCA PRESS

First Edition: December 15, 2016
HC ISBN: 9781939604-101
PB ISBN: 9781939604-118
Library of Congress Control Number: 2016933657

Subject Areas:
Friendship, Multiculturalism, New at School, Hispanic & Latino; Southwest, Calexico, Mexico; Spanglish language.

References:
A Dictionary of New Mexico and Southern Colorado Spanish,
  Rubén Cobos, Museum of New Mexico Press 1987.
Spanglish: The Making of a New American Language,
  Ilan Stavans, Harper Collins Publishers 2003.
The Spanish Language of New Mexico and Southern Colorado,
  Garland D. Bills and Neddy A. Vigil, University of New Mexico Press 2008.
The New Partridge Dictionary of Slang and Unconventional English,
  Tom Dalzell and Terry Victor editors, Routledge 2015.

Manufactured in the United States of America.

To the memory of nuestra amiga
Victoriana Espadas/Vicky González
y su familia, from our family,
PDL

For Olga Guartan,
with appreciation and love,
SLR

"¡Adiós!"

María de la Luz waved to her teacher and skipped along the Calexico sidewalk toward home. Her house sits on the edge of California, right down the street from houses just like hers in Mexicali on the Mexican side of the border.

She strolled through Calexico's downtown, past stores selling the fresh fruits and vegetables her grandmother buys for her, and past the colored candies her grandmother doesn't buy for her.

"¡Hello, **Tío** Ricardo!" she called to her uncle, working at his gas station. **"¿Qué pasa?"**

"**¡Hola** *güisa!* ¿Want to help with the *gaselín*?" he yelled back. "I'm busy fixing this *flate* from your **papá**'s new *picap*." "I can't, Uncle Ricardo. Grandma says I need to go **a la casa directo** after school."

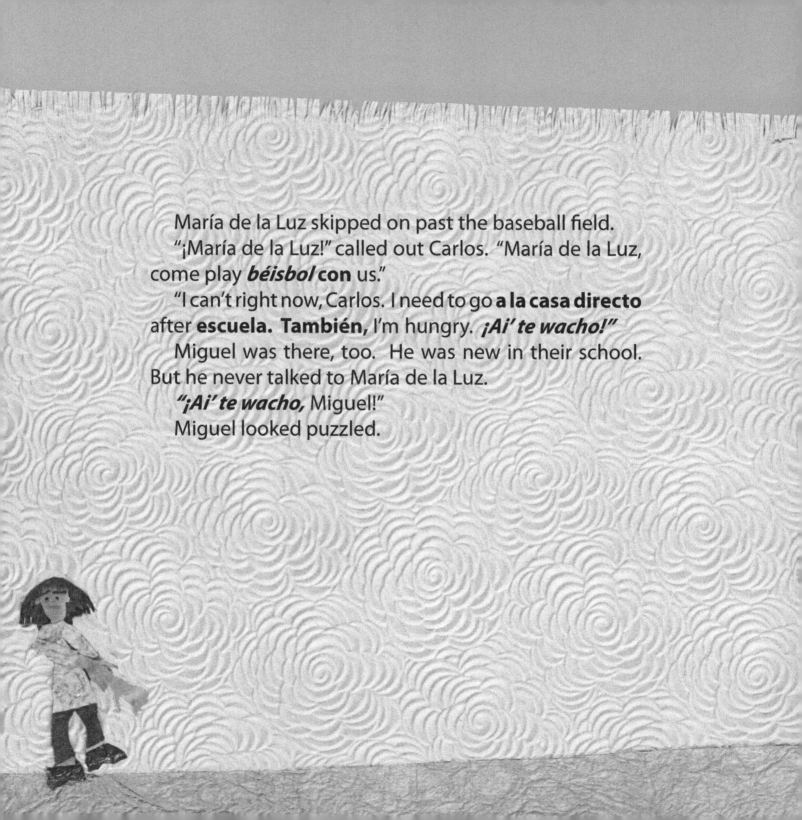

María de la Luz skipped on past the baseball field.

"¡María de la Luz!" called out Carlos. "María de la Luz, come play **béisbol con** us."

"I can't right now, Carlos. I need to go **a la casa directo** after **escuela. También,** I'm hungry. *¡Ai' te wacho!*"

Miguel was there, too. He was new in their school. But he never talked to María de la Luz.

"¡Ai' te wacho, Miguel!"

Miguel looked puzzled.

María de la Luz crossed Main Street and turned onto Third Street. Her dog came running out from her house to meet her.

"¡Amigo!" she called to him. "Let's go get a **hueso** for you from Grandma. I know she saved the bones from the **sopa** she cooked yesterday."

Amigo licked her. While María de la Luz petted him, she noticed an old Chevy pickup truck parked in her yard. It was missing a wheel. Amigo and María de la Luz jumped up the front steps.

"¡Grandma!" María de la Luz called out. **"¡Hola,** I'm home!"

"¡Hola, niñita!" Grandma hugged María de la Luz. **"Dame un beso."**

María de la Luz kissed Grandma. And Grandma smiled.

"¡Grandma! ¿Whose *troca* with the broken *güinchil* is parked in our *yarda?"*

"¡María de la Luz Elena Gómez Rodríguez! How many times have I told you?" Grandma did not smile. "Either say: **¿De quién es la camioneta descompuesta en nuestro patio?** Or say: Whose truck with the broken windshield is parked in our yard? Proper Spanish or English, María de la Luz. But not that Spanglish! **Por favor, dulce."** Grandma did not like it when María de la Luz spoke Spanglish.

María de la Luz sighed and said, "Whose truck is it?" If she couldn't speak Spanglish, English was easier for her. That's what she was taught in school.

"It's your **papá**'s newest toy." Grandma was smiling again. "Are you hungry, sugar?"

"I'm hungry, Grandma," said María de la Luz, poking around in the refrigerator. **"Perdí mi *lonche* at school."**

"¡María de la Luz!"

"Oh, I'm sorry Grandma. I couldn't find my lunch at school. **Perdí mi almuerzo en la escuela."**

Grandma was smiling again. She liked to hear María de la Luz speak Spanish.

María de la Luz found some leftover chicken.

"Grandma, may I eat this chicken, I mean **este pollo?**"

"Claro," said Grandma. She liked it when Maria de la Luz ate.

"Grandma, our *ticha* says *espeliar* . . . Oh! I mean, my teacher says I need to learn how to spell all these words for a test tomorrow."

"There's nothing wrong with Spanglish, **niñita,**" Grandma said as they worked together on her spelling words. "I just want you to speak proper English and proper Spanish. If all you know is Spanglish . . ."

"But, Grandma!" said María de la Luz. "All the kids understand me. We all talk the same."

The next day after school, María de la Luz passed the new boy, Miguel, at the baseball field as she skipped home.

"¡Ai' te wacho!" she called out.

"¿Qué?" asked Miguel.

"¡Ai' te wacho, socio!" repeated María de la Luz.

"No comprendo," Miguel said to her.

"¿No comprendes?" she asked. "It means, see you later, buddy. How come you don't know that?"

Miguel just shrugged his shoulders.

María de la Luz saw her friend Carlos throwing practice pitches.

"That new guy didn't answer me when I said **_Ai' te wacho_** and see you later," she complained to Carlos. "Do you think Miguel doesn't like me?"

"**El nuevo** didn't understand you, *güisa,*" said Carlos. "He's from way down south inside México **cerca de** Guatemala. He doesn't know **Inglés** and he doesn't understand our Spanglish. He **solamente** speaks Spanish."

María de la Luz thought for a minute and then smiled. **"Comprendo, amigo. Gracias,"** she said. *"¡Ai' te wacho!"*

She left Carlos and started to run home. She turned the corner onto Third Street. Her dog came to meet her.

"¡Vámonos, Amigo! Come on, let's go!" She and her dog ran home.

María de la Luz and Amigo jumped up the front steps and ran into the house.

"Grandma!" María de la Luz gave her grandmother a big kiss.

"Grandma, how do you say *'Ai' te wacho'* in your Spanish?"

"¡Hasta luego, niñita!"

"¡Hasta luego, Grandma!" María de la Luz called as she ran out the door. "I'll be right back," she said.

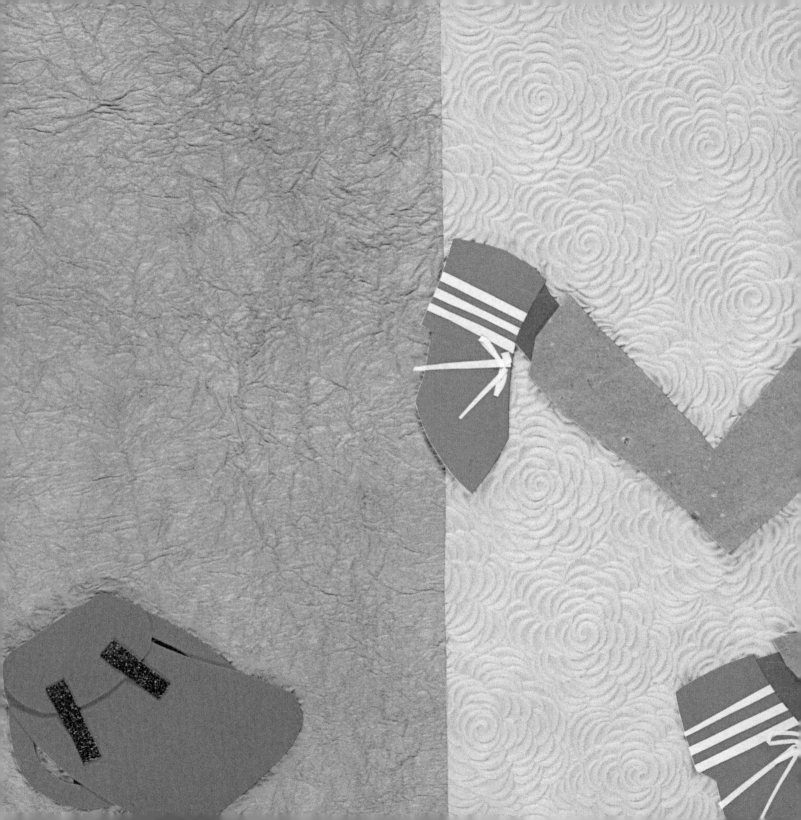

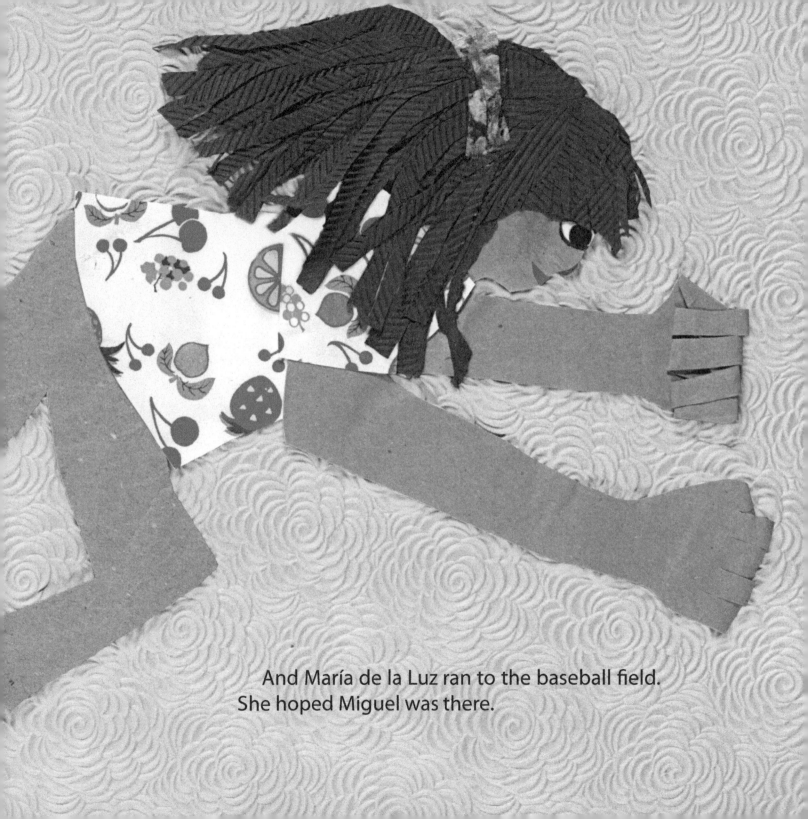

And María de la Luz ran to the baseball field.
She hoped Miguel was there.

See you later!

¡Hasta luego!

¡Ai' te wacho!

¡Hasta luego!

See you later!

¡Ai' te wacho!

Spanglish

Since the mid-nineteenth century, when many **Americano** settlers began moving with their language into Spain's former colonies (now the United States Southwest), Spanish and English speakers have been borrowing words from each other. Spanglish is a rich and creative patois. Here are the Spanglish words and their English equivalent used in the story:

Many Spanglish words, like *espeliar,* are the English sounds with Spanish verb endings attached.

Flate is a direct borrowing and can be used with soda pop as well as tires.

Gaselín is one of those words that came into the region with the product.

Güinchil means windshield; automobile words came West with the machines.

Güisa means girlfriend or good-looking. It comes from sweetheart. In an earlier form it was even closer to the English: *suija*.

Lonche is lunch.

Picap is a word that was created to maintain the tone of the English, as was *béisbol.*

Socio is one of the terms good buddies use for each other.

Ticha is teacher.

Troca means truck.

Yarda can refer to both the land around a house and the unit of measurement.

Ai' te wacho captures the playfulness of Spanglish. The "aye" sound comes from a contraction of the word for "here", **ahí**; **te** for "you"; and the English word "watch" is conjugated as if it were Spanish – to make "I'll be seeing you (here)."

Font and the Depiction of Languages:

To show that languages are mixed in everyday speech, we could have formatted all words in roman. But we chose to use roman for English, bold for Spanish, and bold italics for Spanglish in the formatting of this story. Why did we do so? Since this book is, in part, about language acquisition, we thought it useful to highlight the ways in which people use multiple languages.

Peter Laufer is the James Wallace Chair Professor in Journalism at the University of Oregon. He is author of many works of adult non-fiction including *¡Calexico! True Lives of the Borderland* (University of Arizona Press).

Susan L. Roth is illustrator of more than 50 picture books for children, many of which she has also written. Her collages illustrate *Parrots Over Puerto Rico* (Lee and Low Books), which received the Robert F. Sibert Medal with co-author, Cindy Trumbore.

Previously, brother and sister Laufer and Roth collaborated on the children's picture book, *Made in Mexico / Hecho en México* (National Geographic).

CPSIA information can be obtained
at www.ICGtesting.com
Printed in the USA
LVOW06*2317181216
517873LV00013B/48/P